T0113335

Kavanna, Mermaid Angel Of The Ocean

BREN FREDERICKS

WESTBOW
PRESS®
A DIVISION OF THOMAS NELSON
& ZONDERVAN

Copyright © 2016 Bren Fredericks.

All rights reserved. No part of this book may be used or reproduced by
any means, graphic, electronic, or mechanical, including photocopying,
recording, taping or by any information storage retrieval system
without the written permission of the author except in the case of
brief quotations embodied in critical articles and reviews.

WestBow Press books may be ordered through booksellers or by contacting:

WestBow Press
A Division of Thomas Nelson & Zondervan
1663 Liberty Drive
Bloomington, IN 47403
www.westbowpress.com
1 (866) 928-1240

Because of the dynamic nature of the Internet, any web addresses or
links contained in this book may have changed since publication and
may no longer be valid. The views expressed in this work are solely those
of the author and do not necessarily reflect the views of the publisher,
and the publisher hereby disclaims any responsibility for them.

Any people depicted in stock imagery provided by Thinkstock are
models, and such images are being used for illustrative purposes only.
Certain stock imagery © Thinkstock.

ISBN: 978-1-5127-5333-2 (sc)
ISBN: 978-1-5127-5332-5 (e)

Print information available on the last page.

WestBow Press rev. date: 10/31/2016

KAVANNA, MERMAID ANGEL OF THE OCEAN

K avanna hears a man's calm voice say "the rain will start early tomorrow morning but by noon the sun will be shining bright," and then there was crackling and all was quite. Dare she slip well under the boat so her tail would not splash? She really wanted to listen to what the people on the boat were saying. Through the years Kavanna listened to tales of families sojourning to lands far away so their children would have a new start. Listening to stories of kings that just wanted more taxes paid to them, and stories of famine and destruction was common to hear, for centuries. She would come as close as she dared and listen so intently, learning about the humans and how they managed through the day, and through their lives. Too many times she had seen the war ships battling and many bursting apart and sinking deep into the waters. Diving deep she could see the helpless and she prayed for them. She would scout the sea's floor for any fish that were hurt and try to help them. Fortunately the giant shadows and the noise from the war machines sent most fish hurrying to get far away.

Once a giant ship with smaller boats fastened to the side was headed for a place that Kavanna recognized as a problem, and she realized why she was sent on this mission. The intense cold waters she navigated would not even bring a shiver to the mermaid angel. She knew the mountains of ice under the waters would go undetected by human eyes and she was not shocked at the horrendous cracking sound when the ship and an iceberg connected. Kavanna was ready as she watched the people finally lower the smaller vessels and help people escape. She heard the frantic shouting and the whispered prayers. She brought people comfort in ways they did not realize. Some had peace; some found a stranger's hand to hold onto. Others had sudden warmth, even though they knew the cold and the deep waters would take them. A few of the older ones clutched the crosses that had been worn around their necks for a time such as this. They kissed their loved ones and they kissed their crosses, and said "Jesus". Kavanna prayed for those that had not made their peace with their savior.

She was always ready for her missions and she would pray:" Heavenly Creator, I am here to serve you. Grant me the knowledge of how to follow your commands. Empower me to do your will. I am your servant."

She loved seeing the sails blowing in the wind whisking the sailboats along. Porpoises jumped and swam along side the boats and an invisible mermaid would be swimming in the sparkling water along side the boats also. The crackling would happen quite often now and then a monotone voice would give insight on how people lived on the lands along the ocean. Sometimes a woman on board would bring a baby close to the boat's side and how Kavanna loved hearing the babies laugh! She listened while the boats would float, casting their nets or try to get the big fish with big fishing rods. Sometimes there was soft singing and always there were strange sounds that she had no idea what they were. She had to be careful as they tried to find fish and she would keep hearing them curse or laugh as the big one got away.

The beautiful Kavanna usually does not swim alone. She is a welcoming site with the giant squid and she can swim around their long arms playfully trying to catch her. She once stopped a fight between a giant squid and a sperm whale. Seems the squid was using it's tentacles to hold the whale down. But just by letting the big bossy squid know that she was there put an end to the bullying. Kavanna can sit on coral and watch the tripod fish as they kind of walk along the white sandy ocean floor. She loves to gingerly catch a viper fish and look at the lights inside its mouth. The fish does not mind. The cold currents do not change course, nor does the sand on the ocean's floor show any sign of her being there. Ageless, wingless, long and agile, a gift from God sent as a blessing of help to whatever creature has needs.

Kavanna remembers the beginning of her creation. Her memory starts with Phaysha, another mermaid angel, standing close and singing sounds of praise to their Creator, all while Kavanna's body was being formed. Kavanna was lying in a huge oyster shell and rose out of it as beautiful and glowing as an iridescent pearl. As God's newest angel opened her long black lashes, she knew her own name as well as the reason for her creation. Kavanna was formed into this cluster of angels of the ocean from the moment the waters were separated from the land and all the fish were formed. All of these lovely beings travel the oceans and seas to do the will of their wondrous King.

Kavanna's name has many meanings, but her favorite one is, prepare to enter into worship of the Lord. Swaying and softly floating in and around mounds of sand, small craters, and grasses of many colors is how Kavanna gets to her many duties. While she is silent her inner thoughts are of how wonderful her God is. Kavanna's lower body is patterned with diamond shapes that range from pale blue to the deepest purple and flips the water so that the droplets falling down create the look of white wings. Her body is strong with arms and hands that can grasp. While this lovely creature is swaying about the bottom of the sea, her bright eyes are ever watchful. Sometimes she thinks she has found a ring partially hidden in the oceans' sandy floor, but the shining light is from the sunfish's silvery scales. Every now and then she finds a necklace, or something made from gold and she wears it. Kavanna wears most of the items she has found. She wears gems and pearls from ancient cities that were drowned. From storm tossed shipwrecks, and rejected lover's rings tossed overboard, Kavanna has searched and has found bright golden cuffs and bracelets that she wears on her wrists. The angel's white, soft as silk hair is decorated with emerald and ruby barrettes, and a tiara on her crown is full of tiny pearls and glowing gems which give her presence a royal flair. Each finger has at least three sparkling rings that add to her aura. The shine from her jewelry alerts and delights the fish as they see the bright glow and they know Kavanna is coming!

As good as Kavanna is and her sister clan, there has been evil in the underwater paradise. Their presence is as overwhelming as being caught in the shadow of the sperm whale as it passes overhead. The good and the bad, this is how it has been from the creation of the heavens and will be till the end of all time. The Sirens, as folklore calls the evil mermaid sisters, have used Kavanna as a target for their cruelty. The sinister side of evil, they know they are wrong and just can't seem to try to be good as Kavanna, and her mermaid clan. Kavanna is the easiest to pick on since she wears her treasures. The vengeance began as the Sirens offered a necklace to Kavanna and Kavanna refused their gift. The vile seduction of their provocative voices lured countless sailing vessels and lonely sailors towards their home of rocks formed from black dust spewing from the depths of the coldest waters. Not caring their boats would crash, the men followed the hypnotic spell of the tantalizing song the sisters' voices carried. A swirling purple fog would surround the rocky throne. The lusting captains and deck hands would desire to meet the women who sang the songs that tugged at them. The songs captured them as if a rope had bound the men pulling them to the Sirens. For many the exhilarating and savoring intrigue lured them to an unsuspecting watery grave.

As soon as the vessels were torn apart and all the foolhardy had vanished from the cold bitter waves, the Sirens would slide from their hard couches and go into the depths looking to salvage treasures. Two would find one chest and the hissing started spewing from the ugly mouths and the evil in their eyes would try to cast a spell while their sharp nails clawed in each other's hair. Much scratching happened before one backs away in search of an easier find. Kavanna would never wear jewels that were taken in such cruel ways. One would always find some remark to try to shatter Kavanna's self confidence, such as, "Kavanna thinks she is special to God and can never do anything wrong". "Wearing the tiara has her thinking she is a queen over all the oceans and she is too good for us." Kavanna tries to stay far away from the Sirens and God is merciful in giving Kavanna reasons to stay out of their territory. Good always wins over evil. Their evil remarks are always balanced just a bit as they know if they go too far God will call on His sword fighting angels and they could not fight that power.

Kavanna had heard the story why the Sirens were so mean. The Legend of the Rocks spoke of a time long ago when a lady of the village wanted to have children. The men in the village were mean and dirty. The treatment to all the women was harsh. It seemed the men did not know how to treat even one beautiful woman with respect. The women cringed together vowing not to let even one of these horrible men come near them, even if it meant they would never marry or have children. Time passed and the women started asking about the men in the surrounding villages or even travelers they hoped would come by. Their local men kept all the tradesmen away when they found the women thought of them with contempt. To keep men away the trees were fallen across paths. Boats were punctured so no one could leave by sea. The offended men leached stories of how wicked and evil the women in their town were. As the women grew older and childless their bitterness covered their souls like the fog covered the mountain each morning, Bitterness and hatred in the heart leads one and then another, and then all to an early grave. Their unforgiving spirits led them to cliffs that hovered over the ocean and a group of rocks that looked like smooth beds. As they fell, the cries of the birds and the mist moistened the sound of the screams of the women and it became a powerful cry for love and come hither. The men came in boats hungry for loving and mesmerized by the women's words that were turning into songs to lead the men to the Sirens. The ugly grey fog clung to the rocks and the women so much that the men had no idea how evil the Sirens looked. Being captivated they just followed the songs until their boats crashed into the rocks and as their bodies tumbled in the water they could hear the awful sound of the laughing. Satisfied they had manipulated the men, the women waited till the sea calmed and they swam to find any treasures in the sand. Searching for a twinkle nestled between rocks they grabbed anything that looked like silver or gold and even laughed while removing the dead men's jewelry. The Sirens still haunt the rocks and the ugly fog surrounds them.

Kavanna kept listening, trying to understand what the men were doing in this part of the ocean and she forgot to watch for the net. Silently, the black cloud of netting nested about her and swept her up and onto the vessel. The net was not the only thing that went black, so did the thoughts in Kavanna's mind. She was not able to hear the gasps of unbelief as the men ripped the net anxious to see their treasure. Her thick white hair was drying fast in the bright sun and soon became a cloak covering parts of her nudity. The sparkle of her jewels caught the attention of the staring eyes as much as the sparkle of her multicolored tail. The captain covered Kavanna with his sweater and ordered the men to step away, far away and be silent. The captain and his first mate put the beautiful creature from the sea on a board and carried her below. As Kavanna was unconscious she had no idea that she was being put upon a bed. The captain was concerned about his men wanting to view this captured beauty so he locked the door and slid the only key into his shirt pocket. He would take care of this mystery creation after the boat was locked up in the port.

Chapter 2

P am waited till the truck slowed and stopped and then she jumped down from the safety of the bed and ran down the road. The man size sweater she stole was not thick enough for the evening that awaited her. After many hours of cold she could hardly move and the pain in her ankles was all she could think about. She smelled the corn. The stalks were as tall as she was but they were too thick with leaves to push aside for cover. Besides, the smell was too overpowering to stay the night. Where would she stay? Dew covered you at night and all the grass and leaves would be wet. Pam could not remember staying out all night, but if campers and hunters did, so could she. Of course they had some supplies because they had planned ahead, Pam had no such plans. The almost white ponytail swung while she shook her head, I never had time to plan, just run. Her tired feet and aching ankles inched toward the end of the cornfield and she noticed the large white moon, its rays bringing a bit of welcomed light.

Pam breathes in and knots her fists while saying to herself, "I am running across the field and into the parking lot!" She noticed a small factory and a trucking company beyond the parking area and decided she would look for an unlocked car and take refuge there. No way was she going to get into a dumpster or one of the huge semis. Pam had heard all the warnings about not having cute license plates or leaving jewelry in the cars that would tell a thief that the car belonged to a woman, but she used this info to help find a safe hideaway. Old ladies drive light blue cars at least that seemed familiar. That is the car she would look for. Wearily she looked for signs of a car belonging to an older woman and when she saw the pink crocheted tissue box in the back window, of a light blue Chevy, she knew she had to try the back door-it opened. Stuffing her hands into the pockets for warmth, while she looked for any sign of being discovered, her fingers curled around dozens of bracelets, rings, and hair pins. Immediately, Pam felt warmer and at peace.

Nestled and hopeful, Pam realized her legs really felt restless and she could not explain why, almost like they did not fit her body. Sleep finally came for a short time but upon waking her mind was racing with thoughts. She tried to think of previous nights and all her head did was swirl. She felt like she had just been woken up from a long sleep. She seemed to know what was needed to survive but could not remember how she knew this or how she knew anything, other than what she remembered the voices saying from the crackling boxes.

Elaine says, "Bye, bye Inez and get some rest!" "See you Monday", says a weary Inez as she heads towards her old lady's car. She fumbles for her key as the sun starts to light the new morning. She finds her key and is not surprised to find that she left it unlocked, again.

Inez turns the key and the engine turns on as well as the radio. Pam is awake, startled by all the sounds, especially the radio, "that is like the voices I have heard before!" Pam is also startled knowing the car is leaving the parking lot. Inez yawns and dabs at her hair while she thinks, "something is not right". A short time later the car is stopped next to a tree beside the fence and Inez is glad to be home. She feels strange, kind of peaceful and she prays, "God, I don't know what is happening but lead me on, I am ready!" With half a laugh she goes on to the house. Pam is cold, shivering and she heard the woman, Inez talk to God, so maybe she can go to the door and get help. Pam pushes up with her right hand and coaxes her legs to do the same and finally they obey. Sitting up, she leans forward to open the door. "AHA! " Inez is flabbergasted that she felt she needed to go back to the car and now she sees a young woman in the back of her car. Her heart is beating so fast, could it be Becka? Inez, opens the door and her heart stops, no, not her Becka. "Come out and tell me what is going on!" As Pam's lean body unfolds out of the car's doorway, she is ready to run, but her legs are set on staying. "I am Pam, I need help".

Inez immediately knew this was a time to help and not ask questions. The burly framed woman helps Pam into her home. The door closes and Pam sits on the sofa saying, "thank you."

"I will get you some food", Inez spoke although she was half way to the kitchen. In a few minutes a mug of vegetable soup was in front of Pam. The steam instantly warms her nose and the mug's heat feels so good to her fingers. Inez enjoyed watching the comfort that a mere cup of soup was giving. "I will show you where you can sleep and in the morning you can tell me what is going on."

Becka's room was almost as she left it, a few months ago. Inez pretended to be cleaning the lavender room, but she just could not stop looking for clues as to where her daughter could have gone, and why God why? Becka's clothes would probably fit Pam and there was truly nothing worth stealing, except for Becka's necklace. Why did she leave that, she always wore it. There were more questions flying around Inez's mind. That always happened when she opened the door to Becka's room. Pam could sleep; Inez knew she would be awake most of the night.

Pam woke early and realized she had made it! She was away from danger and she was ready to start her new life. "I am Pam." Somehow that did not sound right, but it was the only name she could think about. As she looked about the room, Inez opened the door and said, "Good morning, come to the kitchen when you are ready. Use the clothes in the closet and drawers, the bathroom is free."

Inez was ready for a new day, a weekend, and was into a prayer when Pam walked in. "Thank you for taking me in." Between sips of coffee and bites of cereal, Pam explains that she was on a ship and the door was locked. She is not sure why she was on the ship but she wanted off so badly when she realized she was being held captive. The captain was giving orders to dock when Pam finally broke the lock and slipped overboard. Even she was amazed at how fast she could swim.

Inez needed to excuse herself as the phone rang. Pam used this time to remember what happened as she escaped. She ducked under the water and swam as if she had flippers and an oxygen tank, as she stayed under for such a long time. Very soon she made it to a tall grassy bank and looked at her legs and feet. She knew they were hers, they were attached, but somehow she wondered where they came from. While touching the rim of her toenails, Pam noticed the rings on her fingers and the bracelets on both wrists. Each finger had at least three rings of gold or silver. Some had stones and even words written on them.

The gold engraved cuffs on her upper arms were the next for inspection, and then her hair for any jewelry and yes, she had a headband. Slipping back the hairband that was tiara shaped, Pam angled it so the jewels caught the light shining through the window. Smiling, she put the band on and examined the rest of her body. She knew things and saw things and although she understood, enough, she felt as if she had just been born. All things seemed different, a bit off kilter. Looking at her reflection, Pam smiled, she liked this new adventure.

Still smiling, she was remembering her pact with herself to like this new life. Inez was looking at all the jewelry Pam was wearing. Last night she could hear a jingle as Pam was led to the bedroom and wondered then what was in her pockets, and now at breakfast Pam was wearing enough gold and silver to buy a third world country. And did the girl ever hear of the three piece rule! Inez wanted to ask the why and how of so many things, but she still had a peace about having Pam here. Maybe it was just that Pam was taking her thoughts away from thinking about Becka. Pam was still explaining, but kind of going in and out of the same story. Tears started trickling from Inez's eyes and Pam saw her staring at a picture. Pam asked as she took Inez's hand, "Who is she?" Inez replied slowly, "Becka, my daughter and I have not heard from her in two months." The tears really flowed as Inez spoke the words out loud. Pam asks, "Is the necklace in the bedroom hers?" Inez nods her head yes. Pam replies, "I wondered why it was there and not being worn." Inez chuckled and said "yes, you would and I certainly wondered why you have on such a collection of rings and expensive jewelry!" Pam's hand went to the hairband and felt the jewels. "Is this wrong that I am wearing my things, I love them!" "Well, it is a bit unusual to wear all that you have and you could be in trouble if someone wanted to steal them." "I have always worn what I have found." "Where would you find golden rings and cuffs?" Pam hesitated a bit too long before Inez broke in and said," You do not have to explain". We really do not have time now any way, we are off to the tea party". Almost laughing Inez really wanted to know where the jewelry came from but she wanted to know even more how Pam picked her car. "Pam, can you at least tell me why you picked my car to hide in?" Pam was delighted to answer this question, "because it looked like it belonged to an old lady and it did!" Inez roared with laughter!

The laughing pair drove a few miles and turned into a shaded lane that led to Elaine's lovely old brick home. Elaine, Inez's sister took in ladies and cared for them just like they were family. Today was the first Saturday of the month and that meant Andrea was bringing her Traveling Teacups for a party! Inez quickly explained that the ladies loved the dainty sandwiches and hand painted tea cups that was part of the company Andrea created, but they each cared for Andrea as much as if she were their own daughter. Most would wear their nicest shawl and broche. Some made sure they had their lace handkerchiefs on their laps. Intentionally vying for Andrea's attention, the now prim and proper ladies would ooh and aah after each sip or bite. The sweet tea lady would sit at the piano and play some of the old favorites the ladies knew from their church days, long ago. When Andrea's fingers hit the first notes of "Amazing Grace", a sing along started. Inez took Pam to the kitchen to speak with Elaine. Elaine and Inez had already spoken on the phone, but Elaine wanted to see for herself why her sister thought this stranger was so wonderful. After introductions and a fresh cup of tea for each, the trio sat down. Pam was calm and knew she was going to be questioned. Elaine could see that Pam was willing to be asked anything and suddenly nothing seemed so important after all. So Pam showed up at night, stowed away in her sister's back seat, wearing men's clothing, and completing her ensemble is a mass of jewelry fit for a queen. But, I like her and she does not seem to be in hiding, thought Elaine. Elaine explained to Pam that she had an offer for her. "I know you need a place to stay and I could use help." "How would you like to help me with my ladies, and in return, you can live here." Inez explained a few things to me last night and if Becka came home and found you in her room, she might leave again. But you can take a few outfits from her closet and put them in your new room. Pam looked at Inez and Inez was smiling, "we can still see each other and get to be friends." Pam was so excited, and she selected one of her rings and put it in Inez's hand. Pam exclaimed, "I can give you this ring in exchange for your help and want to thank you very much!" Inez was shocked at this generous gift and to herself pleaded with God that it was not stolen! The ladies returned to the parlor and joined in the singing, each with a smile of a deed well done. Pam was told to just see to the needs of "my ladies". With a slight giggle Elaine stated she was sure Pam would be kept busy!

CHAPTER 3
THE STORY OF RUTH

Another newcomer joined the ladies at Elaine's nursing home. The name of this quiet worn woman is Mary. Pam walked Mary into the room she would share with Ruth. Ruth was happy to have someone in the room with her. The pink roses on the wallpaper matched the roses you could see out the window surrounding the birdhouses. Elaine not only loves looking after "her ladies" but she was always tending her roses and filling the bird feeders early morning and late afternoons. The women could look out any window and watch the squirrels and birds eat together or admire the latest blooms on the rose bushes. Truly this was a wonderful place if you could not stay in your home. But to have someone to talk to and be friends was something Ruth really wanted.

Mary knew this was her new home. She was like most of the others, her husband had died. She had a bed, good food, willing friends, especially Ruth, but all Mary did was watch the others and then just go to bed. Pam watched Mary, and gave her time and space to get familiar to her new home. Mary had been told about Ruth and how her legs had been removed. She had never seen someone without legs. Mary was born early and had a bit of a weak heart. Since that time her family protected her from anything that could upset her and they kept her from truly embracing life. Her father even found a husband for her, Sal. Sal was new to this country and so happy to find work and friends. Sal loved Mary and promised to care for her forever. He would wake her each morning with a sweet kiss. He would tell her to take her time waking up while he made the coffee. The couple never had children and because Sal loved Mary so much it never seemed to matter. He knew Mary was frail and he ached to hold her passionately, but instead, each night he would take the ivory comb and pull it through Mary's hair. Mary would take out the pins that held up the curls and when they fell Sal would see a lovelier side of his wife and he wanted to caress her skin so much. "Mary, I want to touch every strand of your beautiful hair and I know that will mess it up, so each morning I will comb your hair before you roll it up again. Our secret will be kept just between us of how beautiful you look, just for me, with your hair down around your silky shoulders." Mary would watch his face in the mirror and she knew with the silence and with each long section he was combing, that Sal was praying to God for Her care. He was intent on being gentle with the tangles and delighted when her hair was soft and shining as the sunlight that came in bright through the curtains.

After a beautiful life of loving Sal, he was gone from her. Mary could not handle her life. Who would pray for her and make her coffee? The comb stayed on the dresser for weeks. Inez came to visit and with one look at the lonely widow, she knew to take her to Elaine's home. Quickly, she packed clothes for Mary, and a few items off her dresser and they were on their way. Mary did not even ask where she was going, but recognized the sign by the driveway to Elaine's Home for Ladies.

Each morning Pam would come into the bedroom and help Ruth into her wheelchair, cover her lap with a pretty blanket, and then Ruth would take control of the wheels saying" I can take it from here"! Mary would watch Ruth but never said a word. Ruth was so disappointed that her roommate did not care for her and wondered if she was appalled that Ruth had no legs. Last year was a rough one for Ruth. Diabetes took one leg and when she was told the other was going to be removed she questioned God. "Why would you do this to me? Ruth recently got the phone call that she was going to be fitted with new legs! Ruth loves remembering her time and the giving of her heart to help the last woman that shared her room. The question to God seemed less important as time went on. Maggie, the friend she lost recently had dementia. Ruth would wake her up for breakfast and for the rest of the day, Maggie was as close to Ruth as she could be. Ruth knew Maggie needed her hand when she was frightened, as well as her company when she could not sleep at night. Forgetting her pain by caring for Maggie was the best gift God could have given her, she felt needed, and she was. Maggie's death left a place on a ledge and if Ruth was not careful she would fall over and she knew she would never return. She so hoped this new woman would love her. Her life had changed so much since her Albert died.

A daily routine was started by the roommates of getting dressed and Ruth would comb her short hair. Mary would put on a headband and push her long white, hair back, neglecting the comb Sal had bought her. After breakfast everyone went to the parlor for a time of devotions with those willing to read scripture from the Bible. Ruth loved to read from Psalms and Proverbs as she knew this increased her wisdom. She was not wise about getting inside Mary's heart. Mary still had not done anything but stare at Ruth. After prayer time was done, all the ones in wheelchairs and walkers got on one side of the room and the others lined up across from them. Red, yellow, and green balloons were sent flying across to one another and laughter followed. Arms were stretched as they exercised by trying to catch as many balloons as possible. After a few minutes everyone was ready to go to their rooms. One day as Ruth tried to turn her wheelchair around, the ribbon from a balloon got knotted in her wheel and she struggled to get it loose. Pam came over to help just as Ruth's lap quilt fell to the floor. Mary stared at the empty space where legs should be and she laughed! Ruth was mad, how dare her! And just as she was about to tell Mary how awful she was, Mary stopped her. "You don't understand, I am not making fun of your loss. Mary bent down and retrieved the blanket and placed it in Ruth's lap. "You are so sure of yourself-you can control everything but you still can't hold onto this piece of material? I think I can breathe now since I realize you have a flaw after all." Ruth's hand was on the chair's wheel, ready to turn and leave when Mary said, "I'm going to the same place, let me drive."

Pam was watching and smiling as she walked behind the pair. As she neared Mary's dresser, Pam picked up the comb. " This is a lovely ivory comb". Mary said, "Sal bought it for me. My husband Sal waited in a silk covered chair at a ladies' boutique, while I shopped. He looked silly, holding his hat and not sure what to do with his big feet. I was looking around and trying on dresses and did not realize that he had bought me a gift. That night as I sat by the bed he said the most romantic words to me. Mary, my love, let me comb your hair." And she proceeded to tell how he cared for her.

Pam hands the white comb to Ruth and told Mary where to sit. Puzzled, Mary sat on the corner of the bed and Ruth wheeled over and gently started combing Mary's long messy hair. Tears gently fell on three faces.

As Pam left the room, Ruth was sharing about her Albert and how she knew where to touch him to make him laugh. Tears changed to knowing grins as each remembered another time in their lives. Ruth stopped and then asked Mary, "Why do you think Pam let my blanket fall to the ground?"

Chapter 4
The Great Giveaway

Lynn was not able to go to the tea parties, so the ladies and friends of old, and her family came continuously, night and day. The note on the door stated: I love that you came to visit, but please keep the time to 10 minutes. Since the door was always open, no one saw the sign and Lynn just went to sleep as needed, so that was the newest plan. The wheelchair was in the corner, along with the breathing machine and fan to keep her cool. Her hair was white and the pillows pushed it straight up. Lynn gave up on makeup, and pretty nightclothes, but her aqua nail polish matched her hospital type gown. Gone was her pink ceramic ring that she wore everyday, along with the white ceramic watch. Lynn loved that ring and in its place was an aqua stone on a gold band. To see the pink ring replaced meant she knew she was going to die. Always one to give away anything that she had now became more important to her. She knew that each set of boots, coats, clothes and her computer that kept her in touch with her face book friends would make someone's life a bit better. They were not memorials so she would never be forgotten, no that belonged to her smile that said I love you. The genetic disorder had diseased her lungs and her liver. Prayers have been prayed and we knew of God's mercy. Lynn was getting weaker each day.

Pam watched as Lynn struggled to greet her family. Knowing it was the last time on Earth to hug each one as it was starting to hurt more and more. Pam placed her hands on Lynn's and prayed to their Lord for Lynn to have comfort and peace. As their palms touched Lynn breathed a sigh of release and ages of anger and hurtful memories dissolved. She could not remember them if she had tried. Replacing the bad was feelings of joy and peace. Her soul was calm and her breathing was no longer a struggle. A smile tilted the sides of her mouth and her eyes closed. Those of us, who believe in Heaven, as Lynn did, knew without a doubt, she was there.

CHAPTER 5
PAM MEETS BRENDA

P am woke up just as the sun was lighting up the rose garden. She had a quick breakfast and was off to the barn. This was her day off and Alison, another one of Elaine's helpers had taught her to ride Elaine's old bicycle. She put a water bottle and apple in the basket and turned left at the driveway entrance. Pam was going to see and smell what farm life was like. She enjoyed the barns, both the ones with fresh red paint, and the old ones that had never seen a new coat of paint. The cows had been milked and were lined up at the fence like they were waiting on Pam to come by. The road was curvy and some of the farms were a bit too far away to see what was growing and who was taking care of things. The sky was blue and the grass green and riding the bike was movement she enjoyed. Up the tree lined road was a woman, her neck was down and her face almost touching her blouse. Pam slowed the bike and said a prayer and eased close to the middle aged lady. She looked up and spoke slowly "I don't know you do I"? Pam said "no, but can I sit with you and hear why you are so sad?" Brenda nodded a yes and spoke her name. "Last night I was in a very noisy machine, an MRI, at the hospital. I had to keep my eyes closed and in my mind I could see and hear what seemed like 100 clowns. They were not happy and kept honking their horns. When they could not break through, they found many workmen with hammers and drills and they hammered and drilled over and over and the clowns sounded their horns. Contemporary Christian music played at times and I had ear pieces in my ears but for one-half hour these people tried to get to me and I wanted to scream. I wanted to scream after I was out and safe but I also wanted to keep my sanity. Late this morning I received the news that I have brain cancer. A few days ago, I was told that my liver was enlarged and so were the tumors in it and in my lungs. The cancer in my bones had not changed-for that I am grateful. My doctor said I will try the last chemo that I can and after that I need to call hospice. If you look at me, I look great. If you walk with me, I will walk and enjoy the colors and the smells. I enjoy my life. Look at my hair-it is short-but it has grown, finally. What have I done to deserve this? Why is God not answering my prayers? This seems so unreal, but it is real."

A few years ago I stopped my volunteer work in the local oncology center. When I started the room was new, blue and had large windows-perfect to paint in. My hair had grown back from chemo to what I called the chemo cut and it was just long enough that I did not need a wig. The people in the waiting room knew that I was one of them. I would keep my easel in a closet but bring in my art supplies and sit and paint on canvases for a few hours. I tried to be friends with the lonely. Some men started painting because I let them sit and used my items. I painted what people asked me to and then I gave them the canvas. Hugs, smiles, gift cards were received with such joy. I was blessed and I tried to be a blessing, for six years. Many of the women were in a cancer group and we got together for dinner and even a few parties in my back yard. We called ourselves the Silly Pinks. We cared for each other and I got to know some of them very well-one by one, some of the ladies died. Most had breast cancer that went to organs and then hit the brain. I knew seven beautiful ladies. Most were married, had children and were devout Christians. They smiled, laughed, loved and died. Most of the Silly Pinks are alive and well, but I miss the ones that suffered and died. Why did I make it so long?

How come the ones that had children died? I assumed I would and then had many talks with myself that we were all different. God had plans for us. Just as this really sank in and I stopped thinking it would happen to me-that the chemo was working-bam! So this afternoon when I am having another Silly Pink party-I don't want to attend. I keep thinking about the lovely ladies that will not be here and that I will be next".

Pam took Brenda's hand and said, "You have been a miracle to have lived this long with cancer. Know that God used you to love others." Brenda nodded and said, "I did pray. I knew I needed to love people more. In fact, if someone told me they had cancer, I immediately had love in my heart for them. I knew that if I passed them on the street I would not have cared at all. I prayed for them and listened to them. I cared so much. I had also prayed the prayer of Jabez that my boundaries would be broadened and I would cause no pain. I prayed this Old Testament prayer before my breast cancer diagnosis along with the prayer of loving people enough to die for them. With the cancer I did die, I died to myself when I was in the waiting room. Life was about them and not me. Before the cancer journey started I had listened to a CD of women singing praises to God and I bowed low and sang along. The song was of surrendering and I said to God, "I surrender my body to you." To myself I said, "That was strange, you have already given your body to God. But after the doctor said "you have cancer", the remembrance of that prayer came back to me and it was okay. The first and second journey of finding and taking radiation and chemo and having surgeries was doable. I had a mission. But this is journey #3 and I don't have a clue as to what God wants from me. He has been silent but I still rely on my Lord. Within my first month of my first cancer journey, I had my right breast removed. I will never forget walking out back to my garden and keeping my robe closed, especially on the right side. It was January. I walked out to the rose and grape vines and the thought came quickly, just as the fruit and flowers, I had been pruned. I felt like I had just received a painless slap in the face".

"But again, with this third journey, I have not found Bible scripture that speaks about when you are not healed and you ask to be and do all you have learned to. So I miss my friends, but I also feel like I could be seeing them soon. I just want to hear from God what is going to happen."

"I cried yesterday, laid in bed with the electric blanket on high. I watched a sad movie that had a happy ending. The border of my sheet is wet again. I know that I am a survivor, surrounded by many breast cancer survivors. Some of them are not surviving too well. My tears get stuck and ache to be free. The ladies are my Pink Sisters, my Silly Pink Sisters. One of the ladies said that I was the glue that has started this sisterhood. Being the glue is not what I intended, but this makes me stick to the blessing God has brought to my cancer journey. I just want a happy ending for all of us".

Pam held onto Brenda's hand and hugged her shoulders. "You do have scripture to tell you what to do. We are told not to be anxious or to worry about tomorrow. Enjoy today, this means your friends coming to your party. You are to love them and pray for them. Your friends love you and pray for you. Your surrendering continues on. God has not left you unattended. You have family, angels, and Jesus surrounding you. You have His spirit within you. Sorrow is good, for awhile. Find good things to think of, pure, holy thoughts and think on these. Offer thanks and praise God without stopping. Sing when you can and remember King David danced before the Lord."

"Your friends that have passed are still in your heart. Start a book of their pictures and lives. Some of the ladies at the home have started scrapbooking and that is a wonderful way to remember the beautiful faces. Write them a letter and speak about how their lives influenced yours. I figure you will continue to share your experiences with other breast cancer ladies. You will give them a piece of your heart as well, and this will be giving your journey a purpose. Look at me and smile." Brenda looked up and her eyes met Pam's and she smiled and the tears stopped. Brenda realized that God had not forgotten her, He had brought Pam to her, just when she needed a reason to live."

Pam walked the short path to the creek and left her shoes. She was drawn to the water, any pool, pond, or bathtub. Pam could stay in the tub for hours and she had so much fun winning the swimming contest at the YMCA pool. Her feet started to shake and her legs wanted in the water also. Pam started remembering all the times she felt she belonged in the water and wondered just what God had in mind for her. When she turned to look back at Brenda, she saw a tear fall from Brenda's eye as Pam was walking towards the water. Brenda then came running to Pam saying, "I just can't help remembering my friends. But, now I am planning how I can honor them with the letters and scrapbooking." Brenda gave Pam a hug and invited her to the party, as they were going to have some Silly Pink fun!

CHAPTER 6
LUCY AND LEE

When I think of little Lucy, I also think of the young child actress Shirley Temple. I think of Shirley with her hair in curls and dresses with ruffles. Lucy lived with her mom and her sister Lee, 15 months older, lived separately with her sharecropper father on a rundown farm, not too far away. Lucy's story starts when she was 16 months walking about on the second floor balcony in a small town in Kentucky.

Each school morning, Carrie's son watched little Lucy walk close to the railing of which she could fall through. He was so concerned that he told his mom "we need to go get her and have her live here." One day, Carrie agreed. Lucy's mom who had an attitude problem because she hated her overweight body, made asking anything difficult. Carrie decided she was asking and that was that! "Good morning Lula. I have a difficult question for you. We have noticed little Lucy walking about the railing and we are worried that she will fall through. It seems that you are having difficult times and our family would love to have Lucy live with us. Since we are just down the road you can see her whenever you want." We are not sure of how Lula reacted, but I have a feeling that she knew Lucy needed a better home and since Carrie was so brave she might as well let Lucy go. She could get a better job and maybe a husband.

Lula said, "You might as well grab her up and she does not

have many clothes so I guess you will take care of that also."
Carrie replies, "Yes, I will sew some clothes for Lucy. I will take
her now and we will treat her like a little princess." Carrie not
only sewed new dresses but each dress had ruffles to the knees
and, a 3 inch sash that tied in a big bow in the back. One of the
best matches for the dresses was the bloomers.

Somehow, Lucy got a dog that she named Sunny Boy. This
dog was so protective of the little princess that before Carrie
could wash Lucy's hair, they had to put the dog in the shed. Will,
Carrie's husband, would pick up the dog and put him in Lucy's
baby doll carriage and Lucy would head for the shed, the only
way he would go in. After her hated hair washing, red ribbons
would be put in her hair and this is the type of life she had for 6
years. The Carrie Pilot family treated her like another daughter
and the whole family truly loved Lucy and I am sure she loved
them as well. They probably loved Sunny Boy as he knew to wash
his feet before entering the house and keep his bonnet on.

Meanwhile, Lucy's sister Lee, had no shoes and only one pair
of overalls, dirty ones. There was no one to care if Lee had clean
hair, in fact little sweet Lucy had a big flaw. She was brought to
the farm to see her sister and found her crying. Lucy took one
look and decided she did not like this girl that had no manners
and was ever so loud! Lee took one look at Lucy's fancy clothes
and ways and did not like her sister either and back to the Pilot
family home Lucy went. If only someone had asked Lee why she
was crying-it would have broken your heart.

The following week Pam was taking the bike out again
complete with an apple and water. She decided to try the other
direction and she pedaled for miles. The first little town she came
to had small old homes and lovely ones with huge white pillars that
supported the second floor porch. The windows could stay open
letting the wonderful country air in. Each of the older homes had
gardens with lavender bushes as well as magnolia trees. Pam found
herself sniffing the air and smiling. Then she saw Lucy. Lucy with

her red ribbons in her hair and her sash tied in the most perfect bow. She looked so sweet, except for the sad look on her face. Lucy sees a bicycle coming down the road and she steps out and says "stop". "Can you give me a ride to my mommas? And I need to let my second mama Carrie know that I am going." Pam said, "fine with me if it is fine with mama Carrie." So Lucy nods quickly and runs up the driveway and into the house. Mama Carrie came out and said she wanted to know what was going on and who was this woman. Lucy eyes were running and so was her nose. Pam got off of the bike and explained all she knew, which was not much, and seeing the mess Lucy was in mama Carrie said, "go and I will follow soon." Pam got on her bike and Lucy followed. Pam asked, "Lucy, before you see your mom, tell me a bit of what is going on." Lucy was so embarrassed as she had been thinking how awful she was to ignore her sister that she even hated to tell anyone. "I have been so bad and she cried so hard." Pam got off the bike and carried Lucy to rest under a tree. You need to relax, take a breath. Lucy had never sat on the ground in one of her precious dresses so she lifted up the back and sat on her bloomers. "You told mama Carrie that your name is Pam?" Pam replied, "Yes, but since you might tell me a secret some day can I tell you mine?" Lucy's eyes got so round and just stared and shook her head up and down many times." "I am not so sure that my name is Pam. The name Kavanna comes to mind and I think God brought me here to help people" Lucy never heard a secret before and she said that Kavanna was a pretty name. The tears had dried so it was time to go to mama's. "Mama, mama!" Yelled Lucy as she ran up the steps and mama met her at the door. Pam stayed by the bike and started praying. "Mama, I have been so bad! I am so sorry!" Lula listened, especially to the part of how unhappy Lee was, and dirty. Lucy was talking as fast as she could and Mama started yelling for Bill, her newest husband, to come here and come here now!

Lula told Bill the directions and off for the farm the three of them went. Lee was outside, dirty and crying. "Sissy", Lucy cried while running to her sister. "I am so sorry that I was so mean!" Lee looked shocked! A tear trickled down her pink cheek. No one had ever said that to her! Lee stood still, stiff actually till her chin dropped and one side of a grin appeared. Lucy said, "Sissy you are coming to live with us! Just get in the car." Lee started rubbing her thumbs and remembering the pain. Lee said, "I don't have no clothes or much to go for back in that house, we need to get out of here if we are going." Her father started out the door and Daddy Bill as he just decided his name was going to be, for the girls, was not worried. Bill, lifted one muscled arm and said, "no reason to come further. We are taking Lee and we are taking her now and she will never see you again! " Bill was so rough and just started the car and turned it back down the lane.

Lucy held Lee's hand and said, "you can have my special dress with ruffles and a wide sash with bloomers to match!" Lees' tears cleaned her check as they ran down her face.

Lucy moved back home with her mama, Daddy Bill, and Lee. Mama was so overweight and blamed the kids for that. Lucy always took the blame, then no one would get a spanking. The sisters slept on a sofa couch and like most kids found themselves fighting and keeping mama awake. One night she put a pencil between them, as a line and said not to cross it. It was cold that night and after shivering for a long time, the sisters decided they needed each other's warmth more than they needed to stay away from that pencil.

Pam rode her bicycle over to visit several times. It seemed like after each visit the whole family cared about each other more. Lee was given one half of Lucy's clothes. Mama Carrie and her family were heart broken and not embarrassed to cry. Lucy brought her sister to meet her second family and Mama Carrie was more than happy to continue making clothes for Lucy and for her sissy! Lucy saw Pam waiting for her at the gate and started picking flowers for her. "Kavanna, you are beautiful!" Pam put her finger to her lips and said shush and then hugged Lucy, then they laughed!!!

CHAPTER 7
PAM HEARS FROM HER LORD

Pam has a dream. She is Kavanna and God is telling her how proud He is of the work she has accomplished while on dry ground. Kavanna closes her eyes and presses her hands together and prays," Creator God, you have enabled me to do your will and follow your instructions. By helping others I glorify your name. I know that you want me to return home soon and I ask that you help me finish my assignments. I want to find Becka, then please draw Becka and Inez together while they forgive one another for the painful past. I pray for Ruth to be touched by your mighty love by letting her know the purpose you have for her. I pray for her new legs to lead her in a closer walk with you. I pray your guidance and love over all my friends here. Elaine loves her ladies and I want Lucy and Lee to visit with the ladies and love them like family. The girls' lives have been so limited that being with the older ladies will teach them how to be wonderful women. For Brenda and her friends, let them honor you by trusting you and feeling the Holy Spirit's power enabling them to bring love, joy, and healing to those with cancer."

Pam solemnly says, "Holy are you, good, and merciful. Enhance my gifts that all I do will honor you. Let my voice sing your praise and keep my arms ready to be raised toward you."

Pam in deep reverence continues, "I look forward to returning to my first home when I remember your scripture from the first book of your words: Then God said, "let the waters below the heavens be gathered into one place, and let the dry land appear; and it was so. God called the dry land Earth, and the gathering of the waters He called seas; and God saw that it was good." I am your creation and your servant. I am yours".

CHAPTER 8
BECKA AND KAVANNA GO HOME

Pam has finished helping several ladies finish their lunch. She passes by an empty room except for a very elegant tall blonde walking around. Pam sees her beige stiletto heels and almost becomes jealous. She notices the blonde is speaking on her phone about a flight. Just then, she hangs up and turns around to see Pam. "Hello! My name is Pam."

"Hello to you Pam, my name is Carol. I should be here quite a bit as I am a decorator and Elaine has some special ideas that sound really interesting."

Pam replies, "I admit that I started listening when I heard you speaking to the pilot. I need a pilot that can be trusted with taking me to a very special place and not telling anyone about it." Carol replies, "Why that sounds just like Bob Parrish. He could be a very rich man if he took all the money my husband would give him just to pick up Jackie, my sweet friend and me from my summer home on the coast whenever needed. Bob will be flying us out in less than 2 weeks." Pam replies with "Could I have his number, I need to be out of here in less than 2 weeks also. Maybe we could share the cost of the flight."

Pam headed straight for her room and picked up her phone. Bob answered on the first ring and sounded very friendly." Hello Bob, my name is Pam and Carol gave me your number. In fact, if it could be worked out, maybe Carol, Jackie and I could share the flight since we need to go in the same direction. My situation is really one that I need to trust you and I am sure you want to make sure you are not helping a crazy lady."

"Well, I am curious that is for sure," said Bob. He added, "As far as trusting me, I assure you that as long as you are not handling drugs, or planning to jump out of my plane, we can work this out." Pam said, "could you fly here and I can show you that I do need to jump out of your plane. I understand I need to pay you, so that fee will include dinner." After Bob says tomorrow late afternoon will be fine. Pam said, " I will meet you at the airport tomorrow, thank you."

This time Carol was listening to Pam and Bob. Carol said, "Sounds like you have a secret and I will not ask you to reveal anything, but would you like to join me for a late dinner tonight?" Pam immediately had an idea and said, "I would, but I have been doing some detective work hoping to find a particular young woman." Carol said, "Wow dinner and intrigue! How about I pick you up and we try the Mexican restaurant downtown?" They all agreed to meet at the restaurant at 8:30 that evening.

Pam finished her shift and went to her room to change clothes. Pam had met with Inez three weeks ago and received Becka's necklace. She slid the chain over her black tee shirt, as she had each time she went to find Becka. Of course Pam still had on her headband, armbands, and about a dozen rings. This is Pam and she looks good, and she is off to meet with Carol.

Pam and Carol are seated by the hostess and said their server would be just a moment. They looked at the menu and before they could decide a very upset waitress demanded attention! "How did you get my necklace? I had it made so that I would have something no one else had. Did my mom put it in a garage sale for a quarter? "Sit down Becka and listen", said Pam. Becka was so surprised that she slid into the chair and just stared at Pam. Carol was amused and was wondering what would happen next. Pam unfastened the chain and pulled the necklace around for Becka to take. "I am friends with your mom and since I came here to find you, I would appreciate you calling your mom and have her pick you up here at closing time. We will be here waiting for Inez, so please call her now, and tell her you want to move back home and that you are sorry for wrecking her life." Becka was still staring and must have picked up the angel vibe or something because Becka did not want to mess with this woman. "She tried to speak and all that came out was whoooooo, how, and ok." Carol was really into this now, as Becka called her mom and said what Pam said only with a stutter. Both ladies decided to give their order while Becka remembered she was a server. As Becka slinked away, Carol wanted to know how Pam got so tough. "Let's just say I work for THE MAN and he will not take no for an answer. Both grown women giggled! Closing time was at 10:30 and that is the time Inez flew into the room. Becka saw her mom and the tears started but both went out to the car. About 10 minutes later Pam got a text that said thank you and I love you! Dinner had never been so good!

CHAPTER 9
PAM GOES HOME

Pam was at the airport the next day. She had rented a jeep so Bob and her could go to the pier and then on to dinner. She drove close enough to see Bob get out of his plane, Parrish Airlines. This guy was good looking, a sharp dresser, and definably worked out!

But Pam, having powers could see that this is a man of God and he would do all he could to get her home.

After introductions, they got in the jeep and Bob was curious about the beach towel in the back. Pam drove a few miles to the beach and parked by the pier. They enjoyed the evening sky starting to turn colors from pink to orange and blue to purple-so beautiful.

Pam sat on the end of the pier and Bob did the same. Pam covered her legs with the towel and barely dipped her feet in the water. "So Bob, why do you think I have an unusual secret? Have you thought about what I would do to you if you told the newspapers about me, she giggled a bit?" Bob was still staring at the sky getting darker and said, "If Carol trusts you without knowing the full story, then I am willing to trust you enough to listen. Carol says you have to return home but that takes trusting in the pilot. I admit that I am intrigued" Pam's feet start shaking a bit. Then the ankles and the legs started. Pam quickly moved her self away from the water and made sure the towel was wrapped securely about her legs. Pam apologetically states, "I have lied to you already. Bob, my name is not Pam, it is Kavanna. I cannot prove to you that I am an angel, but I am about to prove to you that I am a mermaid, I am a mermaid angel that God has given a land journey to. Our Lord is now ready for me to return to my duties under the ocean". Kavanna peels back the towel. Bob sees the feet changing into a fish's tail. The ankles are turning colors and the legs are turning purple, blue, gold, and green and the shape is forming that strangely looks like the pictures of mermaids he has seen all his life, but in books!

Bob, still stunned, said, "looks like you need to get home! Let's talk some more while we have diner." Bob pulled the jeep close to the pier and puts Kavanna in it. By the time they reached the restaurant, Kavanna's lower body was back to normal. They order off the vegan menu with Bob still in astonishment. But, he says, "The way the water drop off works is the following way. We drop off Carol and Jackie at their local airport and I refuel. I have to be so many miles out into the ocean to let you off. I can make sure there are no vessels in the area. When I say the word NOW, I will be low enough with the landing gear and flaps down to do a low and slow flight. I want you to remove your dress and hold it tight to your chest. Then, I will unlock and open your door, but you have to remove your seatbelt. Then slide to the wing, and let yourself go, I will circle and hope that I see your beautiful and godly angel mermaid self waving to me." Kavanna nods and says this sounds perfect. As Bob is heading back to the airport he wonders if he can tell Weesie, his wife. She would not repeat anything to anyone; Bob soon gets his wits and knows that this will be between him and Kavanna's boss.

So Pam has about 8 days to say goodbye. She has enjoyed walking, running, swimming, bicycling. But she is ready to swim with her beloved ocean creatures. Her memories of her friends will probably be hidden far back in her mind. Seeing the world above the water has been fascinating. Helping so many and then calling them friends has been so joyful. Where should she start saying goodbye? Pam decides to go find Becka, and she does as Becka is still living with her mom. As she knocks on the door, she sees Becka looking through the window and then Becka opens the door. "Come in, I am so glad to see you." Pam sits on the couch and is so relieved Becka is still with her mom. Pam starts with "I am leaving and going back home. I have a present for you but first I want to tell you something. You had a ring made that no one else could copy. I want you to know that you are the only you in this world. There is no one like you Becka, God only made you, and He loves you. I wear several rings and there are no duplicates to my jewelry". Pam pulls off the first ring on her right hand and hands it to Becka. Pam says, "Now you have 2 rings that no one else has". Becka sheds a tiny tear and gives Pam a hug, and she feels so special. This is how Pam spent her final days. She visited with friends, gave them her blessing and then presented them with a ring of great value. By the end of her eight days her fingers were missing the rings and a few bracelets were gone as well.

Waiting at the airport, Pam felt content and at peace. Carol and Jackie showed up just as Parrish Airlines taxied down the run way. Bob pulled the plane over by the fuel tank and helped the ladies board his plane. Pam had on a dark pink dress and her smile let Bob know she was ready to go home. So after about four hours flying, he taxied into another airport and there they said goodbye to Carol and Jackie. After refueling, Bob adjusted his GPS and headed for the sky. About an hour of flight Pam could see the water nearer and her feet and legs were starting to shake and she knew the time was getting very close. About that time, Bob said NOW, and he opened Pam's door. He looked out the left side of the plane while she slid her dress over her head and then held it tight against her skin. She unhooked her seatbelt and slid to the wing. Her hair had only a moment to fly into her face before she was in the water. Bob turned the plane to the left and when he came to where Kavanna should be, he saw her lift her arms and wave and smile. Bob used the plane to wave back

Acknowledgements

I enjoyed writing this book! This book was left alone all of last year. I had some cancer fighting to do and I gave up on my painting for a year also. Then wam! I started to write this book and paint a few canvases. God must have given me energy and much help in getting so much accomplished. I am still fighting the cancer, only now my brain is involved and that has meant brain radiation and a new kind of fatigue. I hope that I am inspiring someone sitting around with something beautiful to share to please do something to bring it to the world! Give us the chance to hear you and see you and honor God in any way you can.

My dad and mom who are Bob, the pilot, and Weesie are really Robert and Louise Parrish and I do want to thank them for their constant support and love. Bob is everything this book says he is, plus he is my dad.

Many of the characters in this book are named for my friends, but this book would be too large if I put in all my friend's names. I am so blessed with many that are praying for me and loving me. I tell them, you pray for me and I will pray for you-that is a great deal!

The stories are fiction and non fiction, you can probably tell the difference. I love the wisdom that readers can find and that is from our Lord. He is my wisdom and strength. I am very grateful to Him for helping me write this book.

My mom likes to paint and to write stories and so the end

pages are for you to read to the young ones. I even added a story I wrote about mice. Louise, my mom, has written two true stories. Well, as true as a story written by a cat can be. We hope you enjoy them!

Please take your time and enjoy this book. I hope you will be encouraged, entertained, and will share it with someone. God bless you!

I also want to thank Kelly Kimball Huskins. She has come to my rescue. I have known Kelly since she was happy with a piece of dry spaghetti. I came to babysit her and her 2 younger sisters and never saw anyone eat as little as they did. I should have followed their lead. So I have known her for a long time and the whole family is wonderful!

I want to thank the friends who will be surprised to find their names in this book. Sure hope you like this book. I love this book that has something different in each chapter

Thank you for your time in reading what is so important to me.

Bren Fredericks, the author, unfortunately passed away as this book was being brought to print. It was her third battle with cancer. Even though this book is fiction there are threads of actual thoughts and experiences woven in it. One example is chapter 5 called "Pam Meets Brenda" where Bren is actually baring her soul as to what is occurring during her third cancer journey. Bren was a kind, sharing and caring soul that faced cancer with much bravery and a strong faith in the Lord.

Rascle, the One Eye Cat

Hi, my name is Rascle. I am just sitting here reminiscing about the past. I thought this would be a nice story to tell your children, or grandchildren. Well, here goes.

I was born 13 years ago to a really famous lady. Her name was Citgo. I had 3 brothers and 2 sisters. We belonged to an older lady named Louise Parrish. Louise's son was Robert and his wife was Lema Louise. They operated Parrish Grocery and the Citgo station. Now you understand why my mother was called Citgo. She would sit on the railing of the porch of the store. Rain, sleet, or snow, she was always there. People loved her. Everyone would pat her head and buy her treats. My mother was a real star! I know a lot of the customers only came to the store to see Citgo. She did her job well and never would she allow her kitties to sit on the railing.

Then one day our owner, Louise, got sick. It was kind of like Alzheimer's since she would forget things. Louise liked for all of us to sleep with her so all six would stay in her house. It was kind of funny. Robert and Lema had to cook for her and clean the house. My mother really missed sitting on the railing, but Louise came first. She just loved that everyone of us got in bed with her. She fed us all the time and it was only natural that one of us would get sick, on the floor. Well, Robert would put all of us outside. Next Louise would open the window and let all of us back in. Well, here would come Lema with a tray of food and Louise would let us eat what we wanted. So it was eat, eat, and be sick. Be put outside and then Louise would let us back in. It was like a merry go round. When Robert would shoo us out with the broom, we really didn't mind because we knew Louise would let us back in! She would hide us under the covers of her bed. "Mom", Robert would say, "you don't have those cats in your bed do you"! She would say "no, now go on so that I can sleep." This went on for about six months or so. The house was a mess because Lema and Robert could not keep up, so Nita, Robert's sister took my mother, brothers, and sisters. I got to stay with Lema and Robert. I really did miss seeing my family. All the customers really missed my mother Citgo. I really can't complain since I got lots of food. It seemed like everyone in the neighborhood was feeding me.

Then one day, came this mean bird. She was protecting her young. I can't blame her because I love birds and bird eggs, best food in the world! Well, every time she would see me, she would fly low and peck me and it really hurt! One day I was not fast enough and she pecked my eye. I had a terrible time. I didn't want anyone around, so I stayed under the store. I sure didn't want that bird to get my other eye. I stayed away so long that I was sure Robert and Lema thought I had died.

One day I got so hungry that I came out of hiding. My eye had healed by then. I was still so scared of the bird that had pecked out my eye. I would wait until Robert left the store to walk to his home. Robert would say, "come on Rascle". "I will keep that mean old bird from hurting you." He would carry a long stick and wave it in the air. Then after I would eat, he would walk me back to the carport where I had a bed. This went on until the baby birds could fly. But to be honest, I really wanted her baby birds to eat! After all, I am a cat and cats love to eat birds. Had you figured out that I was a cat yet? Oh I am a real cat. In case you have not figured it out by now. This is my first story. I bet you want to know how I am writing this. Well, mystery is the spice of life! Life goes on and I am getting old and stiff. With only one eye I can't roam the neighborhood any more. So I totally depend on Lema and Robert.

But, I have them fooled. I can look real cute. I roll over and when I "Meow", Lema swears that I have said milk. So here she comes with a bowl of half and half. Then here comes Robert acting real tough. He will say in a rough voice, Rascle, I fed you twice today! I just want you to know it isn't so bad being a cat, if you play your cards right. It is kinda like being a woman, you look cute, you pout, then go shopping. Purr, sit on his lap, don't eat much when he is around. You want to look wan and helpless. I know that isn't honest but it got me a new fluffy bed and a heating pad to go under it. It is better to be cute and full and warm than to be hateful, cold, and hungry.

Yours truly, a one eyed happy cat, Rascle

PONCHO, THE RED HOUND DOG

Poncho was a red hound dog that thought he was human. My name is Lema and although I am not an author, I just thought a lot of children would enjoy hearing a real story. Poncho was a real life hound dog who was very smart and acted like he was a real person.

This story was written by Lema Parrish in January, 2009

When our son, Robby, was 12 years old, he had a dirt bike. This could be a story, but today we are talking about Poncho. One day, Robby had probably ridden his bike further away from home, in the woods, than he was allowed to go. Robby came home smiling from ear to ear. He had something in his helmet. A very small red hound puppy was cradled inside his head gear. Robby had found the puppy in the woods and he was very excited! Robby's dad and I would not let him have a dog, but Robby knew that finding this puppy would put a new light on this subject. This tiny dog had no home or parents. We all fell in love with this little red hound puppy dog. We fed him with a small doll's bottle. Robby named him Poncho.

Robert, my husband and I did not like dogs or cats in the house. Well, we couldn't let Poncho stay outside, so he had the run of the house. Poncho was not messy, like most puppies. This dog was more like a child. We took Poncho for walks and he was house broken early. Poncho had a bath once a week and we brushed his coat. I fed him a lot of eggs, so he had a beautiful red auburn coat, almost the same color as my hair.

Of course, I, Lema, had to take care of Poncho most of the time. Robby Jr. went to school, had homework, and football practice. It was just up to me, so I treated Poncho just like a child. My husband and I had a grocery store with a gas station, close to our home. Our business was open seven days a week, from 5:00 A.M. to 9:00 P.M. As you can gather Poncho had to fit into our schedule.

I started training Poncho to set up. I could put three chairs on top of each other and with no problem he could climb up on top and sit up! Then, I started trying other tricks. Poncho would listen really hard and then do the trick. Poncho was a real fun dog, so I put some glasses, without lenses, on him. Poncho had a couple of neck ties, shirts, and a cap, in a dresser drawer. Poncho loved to dress up. I would say, "Poncho, do you want to go to the store?" Off Poncho would run to his drawer, full of his clothes.

I would dress Poncho up and we would go to the store. Sometimes Poncho would get all dressed up and run to the store without me. He would scratch on the back door. Robert would let him in and Poncho would put his paws on the counter like he was waiting on a customer. After a while, people would ask for Poncho. He was a real hit with everyone!

Poncho grew into a large dog. He was really smart and beautiful. We would tie him to a tree between the house and the store, but not in a very tight knot. Well, Poncho would slip away. He would come back and act as if he was tied back up. This dog loved ice cream and bologna. We would hold out the food and say, "here boy, come and eat". But he would not come because he wanted us to think that he was still tied to the tree. No matter how hard we tried, Poncho would not come to us, or the food.

Poncho had a special trait. This boy dog would relieve himself like a girl dog. One day, Robert's sister, Evelyn brought her male dog to visit us. Well, after watching the male dog go potty, Poncho found out how to raise his leg and behave like a real male dog.

Poncho needed a bath. I usually had to drag him to the bath tub. So I said, "Poncho, come and get in this tub!" Poncho peeped around the corner. I had to tell him three times, but he came and got in the bath tub. First, he just stood there and let me give him a good washing. He would never shake water all over me. Poncho was very good natured, but there was sometimes when I had to threaten to get the fly swatter. All I had to do was hit the floor with it or even just threaten to get the swatter. We did get Poncho a big dog house. I painted his picture on the front. One night he started barking. Robert would yell for Poncho to stop barking, but the dog would not stop. Robert wanted me to try to stop Poncho from barking, so I yelled from the window, "do you want me to get the fly swatter?" Poncho stopped barking, but you could hear him ever so softly say, "wulf, wulf". Poncho was a lot of fun and like a child would do almost anything you told him to do.

We have a lot of wonderful memories of our red hound dog. When you have a pet, always treat them like a friend and your pet will be a friend to you.

Lema

The Three Nice Mice
and their Mommee

Mommee, while putting stray hairs behind her huge ears says, "I am sweeping up after you Dustee, again!"" Your tail should be sweeping behind you as you walk then I would not have to!"

Dustee, who looks dirty and probably is walks in leaving a map of where he has been and probably was not supposed to be. Dustee says, "Nothin wrong with dirt and I'm kinda brown anyways. Besides, let me try that sweepin with my tail". He tries but knocks even more dirt around. Then he timidly says, "Sorry Mommee that was not a good idea."

Cookee, who has a tummy as round as a chocolate chip cookie and ears to match says: "Don't sweep up the cookie crumbs-I want them!" And he races to catch the crumbs as they fall from the kitchen above them. His mouth is open wide and bits of cookie are falling all around him.

Lucee, who is dainty with pink ribbons in her hair, giggles and replies, "I know where you hide your cookies! But I don't care, I know that tomorrow is a birthday for the human girl and I know there will be pink frosting and I want it all!"

Dustee to Lucee: "You look like you are a tornado running in circles so fast, but I can outrun you any day!"

Mommee: "Now mice of mine, I love you very much. I want to tell you a story of another mommee that loved her boy.

My mommee told me this story like I'm telling you about this mommee, the prophet Elisha was sent to help."

Cookee with teeth that look black because of chocolate chips in them says, "I know a prophet is a servant of God. God tells him secrets and lets him have super powers. I want to be a prophet! But, can I still have cookies?"

Mommee smiles and says, "Now listen closely my little ones. There was this Mommee that was poor and did not have any food. She needed money to pay what they owed to people and so her son could stay at home with her. The prophet told the son to gets lots of pots from her neighbors. Her son got little pots and big pots. She poured what little oil she had into the pots and the oil poured and poured until all the pots were full! All this mommee had to do was trust in God and she did. They sold the oil and paid their bills and still had money to buy food. This is just one story in the Bible of the miracles that God can do!"

Lucee says, "Why did they need oil?" Mommee replies, "You have watched the upstairs lady cook. She puts oil in the pans first to keep meat from sticking. I have seen her put oil in her baked breads and other foods. Back in the Bible day's people picked olives from the trees and put them in a machine that got out all of the oil. The oil is so important; it is touched on sick people when they are getting prayer."

Dustee is licking his fingers and says, "I remember the story you told about the ten unmarried ladies needing oil for their lamps. They needed to be ready for the bridegroom, and a great party." Not all the ladies had oil and they were called foolish." "Party!" exclaims Dustee, "I almost forgot there will be a party tomorrow with pink icing falling through the floor right over me!"

Mommee says, "Little mice, this is an Old Testament story about the New Testament Jesus as He is the bridegroom and we, the church, are His bride. You keep remembering the stories so you can tell them to your little mice. Now let me get you tucked into your beds." "I am cold and I want to get under covers."

"Burr!" My feet are so cold," says Mommee as she joins her young mice and starts to sleep. But, in the middle of the night the little mice hear coughing, sniffing and sneezing coming from Mommee. All at once the 3 little mice are up and running to their Mommee who appears to be still asleep in their small basement room under the upstairs kitchen.

Lucee says, "I am touching Mommee's head and it is very hot. But, her hands are so cold!"

Dustee replies, "She is coughing so loud, but will not wake up! I am scared."

"We need to trust Jesus and not be scared. He will help us just like God sent the prophet to help that poor woman and fill her pots with oil," says Lucee. Cookee replied, "I trust Jesus and I am a prophet! I don't have pots of oil, but I have sacks of warm cookies! See, I hid them behind the furnace way across the room and they are warm." Dustee quickly replied, "Let's put them over Mommee on her blanket!" "I will put the melted warm chocolate chips on top of the cookies," replied Lucee.

Soon, after covering Mommee, Dustee noticed something different and said, "Mommee is not coughing anymore and I think she is smiling."

Later, Mommee under the warm cookies with the chocolate chip covering was feeling much better and having stopped coughing opened her eyes and said, "My three mice, my three babies I want all of you to get under my cookie blanket and sleep with me tonight. We will truly have sweet dreams as God has provided for our needs. Instead of oil we received cookies and chocolate!"

Printed in the United States
By Bookmasters